The
Trouble
with
Tink

The Trouble with Tink

WRITTEN BY
KIKI THORPE

ILLUSTRATED BY
JUDITH HOLMES CLARKE
& THE DISNEY STORYBOOK ARTISTS

HarperCollins *Children's Books*

First published in the USA by Disney Press,
114 Fifth Avenue, New York, New York, 10011-5690.

First published in Great Britain in 2006
by HarperCollins Children's Books.
HarperCollins Children's Books is a division of
HarperCollins Publishers,
77 - 85 Fulham Palace Road, Hammersmith, London, W6 8JB.

The HarperCollins Children's Books website is
www.harpercollinschildrensbooks.co.uk

938-0-00-720930-9

0-00-720930-4

4

Printed and bound in Great Britain by Clays Ltd,
St Ives plc.

Visit disneyfairies.com

All About Fairies

IF YOU HEAD toward the second star on your right and fly straight on till morning, you'll come to Never Land, a magical island where mermaids play and children never grow up.

When you arrive, you might hear something like the tinkling of little bells. Follow that sound and you'll find Pixie Hollow, the secret heart of Never Land.

A great old maple tree grows in Pixie Hollow, and in it live hundreds of fairies and sparrow men. Some of them can do water magic, others can fly like the wind, and still others can speak to animals. You see, Pixie Hollow is the Never fairies' kingdom, and each fairy who lives there has a special, extraordinary talent.

Not far from the Home Tree, nestled in the branches of a hawthorn, is Mother Dove, the most magical creature of all. She sits on her egg, watching over the fairies, who in turn watch over her. For as long as Mother Dove's egg stays well and whole, no one in Never Land will ever grow old.

Once, Mother Dove's egg *was* broken. But we are not telling the story of the egg here. Now it is time for Tinker Bell's tale...

The Trouble with Tink

1

ONE SUNNY, BREEZY afternoon in Pixie Hollow, Tinker Bell sat in her workshop, frowning at a copper pot. With one hand, she clutched her tinker's hammer, and with the other, she tugged at her blond fringe, which was Tink's habit when she was thinking hard about something. The pot had been squashed nearly flat on one side. Tink was trying to determine how to tap it to make it right again.

All around Tink lay her tinkering tools: baskets full of rivets, scraps of tin, pliers, iron wire, and swatches of steel wool for scouring a pot until it shone. On the walls hung portraits of some of the pans and ladles and washtubs Tink had mended. Tough jobs were always Tink's favourites.

Tink was a pots-and-pans fairy, and her greatest joy came from fixing things. She loved anything metal that could be cracked or dented. Even her workshop was made from a teakettle that had once belonged to a Clumsy.

Ping! Ping! Ping! Tink began to pound away. Beneath Tink's hammer the copper moved as easily as if she were smoothing the folds in a blanket.

Tink had almost finished when a shadow fell across her worktable. She looked up and saw a dark figure silhouetted in the sunny doorway. The edges of the silhouette sparkled.

"Oh, hi, Terence. Come in," said Tink.

Terence moved out of the sunlight and into the room, but he continued to shimmer. Terence was a dust-talent sparrow man. He measured and handed out the fairy dust that allowed Never Land's fairies to fly and do their magic. As a result, he was dustier than most fairies, and he sparkled all the time.

"Hi, Tink. Are you working? I mean, I see you're working. Are you almost done? That's a nice pot," Terence said, all in a rush.

"It's Violet's pot. They're dyeing spider silk tomorrow, and she needs it for boiling the dye," Tink replied. She looked eagerly at Terence's hands and sighed when she saw that they were empty. Terence stopped by Tink's workshop nearly every day. Often he brought a broken pan or a mangled sieve for her to fix. Other times, like now, he just brought himself.

"That's right, tomorrow is dyeing day," said Terence. "I saw the harvest talents bringing in the blueberries for the dye earlier. They've got a good crop this year, they should get a nice deep blue colour..."

As Terence rambled on, Tink looked longingly at the copper pot. She picked up her hammer, then reluctantly put it back down. *It would be rude to start tapping right now,* she thought. Tink liked talking to Terence. But she liked tinkering more.

"Anyway, Tink, I just wanted to let you know that they're starting a game of tag in the meadow. I thought maybe you'd like to join in," Terence finished.

Tink's wing tips quivered. It had been ages since there had been a game of fairy tag. Suddenly, she felt herself bursting with the desire to play, the way you fill up with a sneeze just before it explodes.

She glanced down at the pot again.

The dent was nearly smooth. Tink thought she could easily play a game of tag and still have time to finish her work before dinner.

Standing up, she slipped her tinker's hammer into a loop on her belt and smiled at Terence.

"Let's go," she said.

When Tink and Terence got to the meadow, the game of tag was already in full swing. Everywhere spots of bright colour wove in and out of the tall grass as fairies darted after each other.

Fairy tag is different from the sort of tag that humans, or Clumsies, as the fairies call them, play. For one thing, the fairies fly rather than run. For another, the fairies don't just chase each other until one is tagged "it." If that were the case, the fast-flying-talent fairies would win every time.

In fairy tag, the fairies and sparrow men all use their talents to try to win. And when a fairy is tagged, by being tapped on her head and told "Choose you," that fairy's whole talent group – or at least all those who are playing – becomes "chosen." Games of fairy tag are large, complicated, and very exciting.

As Tink and Terence joined the game, a huge drop of water came hurtling through the air at them. Terence ducked, and the drop splashed against a dandelion behind him. The water-talent fairies were "chosen," Tink realised.

As they sped through the tall grass, the water fairies hurled balls of water at the other fairies. When the balls hit, they burst like water balloons and dampened the fairies' wings. This slowed them down, which helped the water fairies gain on them.

Already the other talents had organised their defence. The animal-talent fairies, led by Beck and Fawn, had rounded up a crew of chipmunks to ride when their wings got too wet to fly. The light-talent fairies bent the sunshine as they flew through it, so rays of light always shone in the eyes of the fairies chasing them. Tink saw that the pots-and-pans fairies had used washtubs to create makeshift catapults. They were trying to catch the balls of water and fling them back at the water fairies.

As Tink zipped down to join them, she heard a voice above her call, "Watch out, Tinker Bell! I'll choose you!" She looked up. Her friend Rani, a water-talent fairy, was circling above her on the back of a dove. Rani was the only fairy in the kingdom who didn't have wings. She'd cut hers off to help save Never Land when Mother Dove's egg had been destroyed. Now Brother Dove did her flying for her.

Rani lifted her arm and hurled a water ball. It wobbled through the air and splashed harmlessly on the ground, inches away from Tink. Tink laughed, and so did Rani.

"I'm such a terrible shot!" Rani cried happily.

Just then, the pots-and-pans fairies fired a catapult. The water flew at Rani and drenched her. Rani laughed even harder.

"Choose you!"

The shout rang through the meadow. All the fairies stopped midflight and turned. A water-talent fairy named Tally was standing over Jerome, a dust-talent sparrow man. Her hand was on his head.

"Dust talent!" Jerome sang out.

Abruptly, the fairies rearranged themselves. Anyone who happened to be near a dust-talent fairy immediately darted away. The other fairies hovered in the air, waiting to see what the dust talents would do.

Tink caught sight of Terence near a tree stump a few feet away. Terence grinned at her. She coyly smiled back – and then she bolted. In a flash, Terence was after her.

Tink dove into an azalea bush. Terence was right on her heels. Tink's sides ached with laughter, but she kept flying. She wove in and out of the bush's branches. She made a hairpin turn around a thick branch. Then she dashed toward an opening in the leaves and headed back to the open meadow.

But suddenly, the twigs in front of her closed like a gate. Tink skidded to a stop and watched as the twigs wrapped around themselves. With a flick of fairy dust, Terence had closed the branches of the bush. It was the simplest magic. But Tink was trapped.

She turned as Terence flew up to her.

"Choose you," he said, placing his hand on her head. But he said it softly. None of the rest of the fairies could have heard.

Just then, a shout rang out across the meadow: "Hawk!"

At once, Tink and Terence dropped down under the azalea bush's branches. Through the leaves, Tink could see the other fairies ducking for cover. The scout who had spotted the hawk hid in the branches of a nearby elm tree. The entire meadow seemed to hold its breath as the hawk's shadow moved across it.

When it was gone, the fairies waited a few moments, then slowly came out of their hiding places. But the mood had changed. The game of tag was over.

Tink and Terence climbed out of the bush.

"I must finish Violet's pot before dinner," Tink told Terence. "Thank you for telling me about the game."

"I'm really glad you came, Tink," said Terence. He gave her a sparkling smile, but Tink didn't see it. She was already flying away, thinking about the copper pot.

Tink's fingers itched to begin working

again. As she neared her workshop, she reached for her tinker's hammer hanging on her belt. Her fingertips touched the leather loop.

Tink stopped flying. Frantically, she ran her fingers over the belt loop again and again. Her hammer was gone.

2

Tink skimmed over the ground, back the way she'd come. Her eyes darted this way and that. She was hoping to catch a glimmer of metal in the tall grass.

"Fool," Tink told herself. "You foolish, foolish fairy."

When she reached the meadow, her heart sank. The trees on the far side of the meadow cast long shadows across the ground. To Tink, the meadow looked huge, like a vast jungle of waving grass and wildflowers. How would she ever find her hammer in there?

Just then, her eyes fell on the azalea bush. *Of course!* Tink thought. *I must have dropped it when I was dodging Terence.*

Tink flew to the bush. She checked the

ground beneath it and checked each branch. She paid particular attention to the places where a pots-and-pans fairy's hammer might get caught. Then she checked them again. And again. But the hammer was nowhere in sight.

Fighting back tears, Tink flew across the open meadow. She tried to recall her zigzagging path in the tag game. Eventually she gave that up and began to search the meadow inch by inch, flying close to the ground. She parted the petals of wild-flowers. She peered into rabbit burrows. She looked everywhere she could think of, even places she knew the hammer couldn't possibly be.

As Tink searched, the sun sank into a red pool on the horizon, then disappeared. A thin sliver of moon rose in the sky. The night was so dark that even if Tink had flown over the hammer, she wouldn't have been able to see it. But the hammer was already long gone. A Never crow had spotted it hours before and, attracted by its shine, had carried it off to its nest.

The grass was heavy with dew by the time Tink slowly started back to the Home Tree. As she flew, tears of frustration rolled down her cheeks. She swiped them away. *What will I do without my hammer?* Tink wondered. It was her most important tool. She thought of the copper pot waiting patiently for her in her workshop, and more tears sprang to her eyes.

It might seem that it should have been easy for Tink to get another tinker's hammer, but in fact, it was not. In the fairy kingdom, there is just the right amount of everything; no more, no less. A tool-making fairy would need Never iron to make a new hammer. And a mining-talent fairy would have to collect the iron. Because their work was difficult, the mining-talent fairies only mined once in a moon cycle, when the moon was full. Tink eyed the thin silver slice in the sky. Judging from the moon, that wouldn't be for many days.

For a pots-and-pans fairy, going many days without fixing pots or pans would be like not eating or sleeping. To Tink, the idea was horrible.

But that wasn't the only reason she was crying. Tink had a secret. She *did* have a spare hammer. But it was at Peter Pan's hideout – she had accidentally left it there quite a while before. And she was terribly scared about going back to get it.

Tink got back to the Home Tree, but she was too upset to go inside and sleep. Instead, she flew up to the highest branch and perched there. She looked up at the stars and tried to figure out what to do.

Tink thought about Peter Pan: his wild red hair, his freckled nose turned up just so, his eyes that looked so happy when he laughed. She remembered the time that she and Peter had gone to the beach to skip rocks on the lagoon. One of the rocks had accidentally nicked a mermaid's tail as she dove beneath the water. The mermaid had scolded them so ferociously that Peter and Tink had fled laughing all the way to the other side of the island.

Tink's heart ached. Remembering Peter Pan was something she almost never let herself do. Since he had brought the

Wendy to Never Land, Tink and Peter had hardly spoken.

No, Tink decided. She couldn't go to Peter's for the spare hammer. It would make her too sad.

"I'll make do without it," she told herself. What was a hammer, after all, but just another tool?

3

TINK SLEPT FITFULLY that night and woke before the other fairies. As the sky began to get lighter, she crept out of the Home Tree and flew down to the beach.

In one corner of the lagoon, there was a small cave that could only be entered at low tide. Tink flew in and landed on the damp ground. The floor of the cave was covered with sea-polished pebbles. This was where Peter had come to get stones for skipping on the water, Tink remembered.

Tink carefully picked her way through the rocks. Many of them were as big as her head. They were all smooth and shiny with seawater.

At last Tink picked up a reddish pebble the size and shape of a sunflower seed. She hefted it once into the air and caught it again.

"This might work," Tink said aloud into the empty cave.

Might work, her voice echoed back to her.

As the tide rose and the waves began to roll in, Tink flew out of the cave, gripping the pebble in her fist.

Back in her workshop, Tink used iron wire to bind the flat side of the rock to a twig. With a pinch of fairy dust, she tightened the wires so the rock was snug against the wood. She held up her makeshift hammer and looked at it.

"It's not so bad," she said. She tried to sound positive.

Taking a deep breath, Tink began to tap the copper pot.

Clank! Clank! Clank! Tink winced as the horrible sound echoed through her workshop. With each blow, the copper pot seemed to shudder.

"I'm sorry, I'm sorry!" Tink whispered to the pot. She tried to tap more gently.

The work took forever. Each strike with the pebble hammer left a tiny dent. Slowly, the bent copper straightened out. But the pot's smooth, shiny surface was now as pitted and pockmarked as the skin of a grapefruit.

Tink fought back tears. *It's no good*, she thought. *This pebble doesn't work at all!*

Tink raised her arm to give the pot one last tap. Just then, the pebble flew off the stick and landed with a clatter in a pile of tin scrap, as if to say it agreed.

Suddenly, the door of Tink's workshop burst open and a fairy flew in. She wore a gauzy dress tie-dyed in a fancy pattern of blues and greens. Her cheeks were bright splotches of pink. Corkscrews of curly red hair stood out in all directions from her head, and her hands were stained purple with berry juice. She looked as if she had been painted using all the colours in a watercolour box. It was Violet, the pot's owner, a dyeing-talent fairy.

"Tink! Thank goodness you're almost done with the... Oh!" Violet exclaimed. She stopped and stared. Tink was standing over the copper pot, gripping a twig as if she planned to beat it like a drum.

"Oh, Violet, hi. Yes, I'm, er... I'm done with the pot. That is, mostly," Tink said. She put down the twig. With the other hand, she tugged nervously at her fringe.

"It looks... uh... " Violet's voice trailed off as she eyed the battered pot. Tink was the best pots-and-pans fairy in the kingdom. Violet didn't want to sound as if she was criticising her work.

"It needs a couple of touch-ups, but I fixed the squashed part," Tink reassured her. "It's perfectly good for boiling dye in. We can try it now if you like."

The door of Tink's workshop opened again. Terence came in, carrying a ladle that was so twisted it looked as if it had been tied in a knot.

"Hi, Tink! I brought you a ladle to fix!" he called out. "Oh, hello, Violet! Dropping off?" he asked as he spied the copper pot.

"No... er, picking up," Violet said worriedly.

"Oh," said Terence. He looked back at the pot in surprise.

Tink filled a bucket with water from a rain barrel outside her workshop and brought it over to her worktable. As Violet and Terence watched, she poured the water into the copper pot.

"See?" Tink said to Violet. "It's good as – "

Just then, they heard a metallic creaking sound. Suddenly – *plink, plink, plink, plink!* One by one, tiny streams of water burst through the damaged copper. The pot looked more like a watering can than something to boil dye in.

"Oh!" Violet and Terence gasped. They turned to Tink, their eyes wide.

Tink felt herself blush, but she couldn't tear her eyes away from the leaking pot. She had never failed to fix a pot before, much less made it worse than it was when she got it.

The thing was, no fairy ever failed at her talent. To do so would mean you weren't really talented at all.

4

AFTER A LONG, awkward silence, Violet closed her mouth, cleared her throat, and said, "I can probably share a dye pot with someone else. I'll come back and get this later." With a last confused glance at Tink, she hurried out the door.

Terence was also confused, but he was in no hurry to leave. He set the twisted ladle down on Tink's workbench.

"Tink, you look tired," he said gently.

"I'm not tired," said Tink.

"Maybe you need to take a break," Terence suggested. But he wasn't at all sure what Tink needed. "Why don't we fly to the tearoom? On my way here, I smelled pumpkin muffins baking in the kitchen. They smelled deli – "

"I'm not hungry," Tink interrupted, although she was starving. She hadn't had breakfast, or dinner the night before. But the talents always sat together in the tearoom. Tink didn't feel like sitting at a table with the other pots-and-pans fairies right now.

Suddenly, Tink was irritated with Terence. If he hadn't told her about the tag game, she never would have lost her hammer. Tink knew she wasn't being fair. But she was upset and embarrassed, and she wanted someone to blame.

"I can't talk today, Terence," she snapped. She turned toward a pile of baking tins that needed repair and tugged at her fringe. "I have a lot of work, and I'm already behind."

"Oh." Terence's shoulders sagged. "Just

let me know if you need anything," he said, and headed for the door. "Bye, Tink."

As soon as Terence was gone, Tink flew to a nearby birch tree where a carpenter-talent sparrow man worked and asked if she could borrow his hammer. The sparrow man agreed, provided that she brought it back in two days' time. He was in the middle of cutting oak slats for some repairs in the Home Tree, he said, and wouldn't need the hammer until he was through. Tink promised she would.

Two days. Tink didn't know what she'd do after that. But she wasn't going to think about it, she decided. Not just yet.

When Tink entered her empty workshop, something seemed different. There was a sweet smell in the air. Then she spied a plate with a pumpkin muffin on it and a cup of buttermilk on her workbench.

Terence, Tink thought. She was sorry that she'd snapped at him earlier.

The muffin was moist, sweet, and still warm from the oven, and it melted on her tongue. The buttermilk was cool and tart. As soon as she'd eaten, Tink felt better.

She picked up the carpenter's hammer and began to work on a stack of pie pans. The pans weren't cracked or dented, but Dulcie, the baking-talent fairy who'd brought them to her, complained that the pies she baked in them kept burning. Tink thought it had something to do with the pans' shape, or maybe the tin on the bottom of the pans was too thin.

The carpenter's hammer was almost twice as big as her tinker's hammer. Holding it in her hand, Tink felt as clumsy as a Clumsy.

Still, she had to admit that it was much better than the pebble.

Tink worked slowly with the awkward hammer. She reshaped the pie pans, then added an extra layer of tin to the bottom of each one. When she was done, she looked over her work.

It's not the best job I've ever done, she thought. *But it's not so bad, either.*

Tink gathered the pie pans into a stack and carried them to Dulcie. Dulcie was delighted to have them back.

"Don't miss tea this afternoon, Tink," she said with a wink as she brushed flour from her hands. "We're making strawberry pie. I'll save you an extra-big slice!"

On the way back to her workshop, Tink ran into Prilla, a young fairy with a freckled nose and a bouncy nature. Prilla always did cartwheels and handsprings when she was excited about something.

"Tink!" Prilla cried, bounding over to her. "Did you hear?"

"Hear what?" asked Tink.

"About Queen Ree's tub," Prilla told her. Ree was the fairies' nickname for their queen, Clarion. "It's sprung a leak. The queen's whole bath trickled out while she was washing this morning."

Tink's eyes widened. The bathtub was one of Queen Ree's most prized possessions. It was the size of a coconut shell and made of Never pewter, with morning glory leaves sculpted into its sides. The tub rested on four feet shaped like lions' paws, and there were two notches at the back where the queen could rest her wings to keep them dry while she took her bath.

Tink's fingers twitched. She would love to work on the bathtub.

"The queen's attendants looked all over, but they couldn't spot the leak. I thought of you when I heard, Tink," Prilla said. "Of course, Queen Ree will want you to fix it. You're the best." Prilla grinned at Tink and did a handspring.

Tink grinned back, showing her deep dimples. It was the first time she'd smiled since she lost her hammer. "I hope so, Prilla. It would be quite an honour to work on the queen's tub," she replied.

Prilla turned a one-handed cartwheel and flew on. "See you later, Tink!" she called.

Tink thought about the queen's tub all afternoon as she fixed the spout on a tea-kettle that wouldn't whistle. What kind of leak could it be? A hairline crack? Or a pinprick hole? Tink smiled, imagining the possibilities.

By the time Tink had finished fixing the kettle, it was nearly teatime.

"They'll need this in the kitchen," Tink said to herself as she buffed the tea kettle with a piece of suede. She would take it to the kitchen, then go to the tearoom for strawberry pie. Tink's stomach rumbled hungrily at the thought. Strawberry was one of her favourite kinds of pie.

But when she got to the kitchen, a horrible smell greeted her. Tink quickly handed the teakettle to one of the cooking-talent fairies and held both hands to her nose. "What is that smell?" she asked the fairy. "It's not strawberry pie."

But the fairy just gave her a strange

look and hurried off to fill the teakettle with water.

Tink made her way through the kitchen until she found Dulcie. She was standing over several steaming pies that had just been pulled from the oven. She looked as if she might cry.

"Dulcie, what's going on?" Tink asked.

As soon as Dulcie saw Tink, her forehead wrinkled. The wrinkles made little creases in the flour on her skin, which made the lines seem even deeper.

"Oh, Tink. I don't know how to tell you this," Dulcie said. "It's the pies. They're all coming out mincemeat."

Tink turned and looked at the steaming pies. That was where the horrible smell was coming from.

"We tried everything," Dulcie went on.

"When the strawberry came out all wrong, we tried plum. When that didn't work, we tried cherry. We even tried pumpkin. But every time we pulled the pies out of the oven, they'd turned into mincemeat." Now Dulcie's chin wrinkled like a walnut as she struggled to hold back tears. Her whole face was puckered with worry.

This was indeed a kitchen disaster. Fairies hate mincemeat. To them it tastes like burned broccoli and old socks.

"Is there something wrong with the oven?" Tink asked Dulcie. She didn't know much about ovens. But if there was something metal in it, she could probably fix it.

Dulcie swallowed hard.

"No, Tink," she said. "It's the pans you fixed. Only the pies baked in those pans are the ones that get spoiled."

5

TINK'S MIND REELED. She took a step back from Dulcie. But before she could say anything, a shrill whistle split the air.

The tea water had boiled. A cooking-talent sparrow man hurried over to lift the kettle off the fire. Expertly, the sparrow man poured the water into the teacups until there wasn't a drop left.

But the teakettle continued to shriek. The sparrow man lifted the kettle's lid to let out any steam that might have been caught inside. A puff of steam escaped, but the kettle still whistled on. Without pausing, it changed pitch and began to whistle a lively, earsplitting melody.

All the fairies in the kitchen, including Tink, covered their ears. Several fairies from other talents who were in the tearoom poked their heads in the door of the kitchen.

"What's all that noise?" a garden-talent fairy asked one of the baking-talent fairies.

"It's the teakettle, the one that just wouldn't whistle," the baking-talent fairy replied. She winced as the kettle hit a particularly high note. "Tink fixed it, and now it won't shut up!"

Twee-twee-tweeeeeeeeee! the teakettle shrieked cheerfully, as if confirming that what she'd said was true. The fairies cringed and clamped their hands more tightly against their ears.

"And the pie pans Tink fixed aren't any good, either," another baking-talent fairy noted over the noise. "Every pie baked in them turns into mincemeat!"

A murmur went around the room. What could this mean? the other fairies wondered. Was it some kind of bad joke? Everyone turned and looked at Tink.

Tink stared back at them, blushing so deeply her glow turned orange. Then, without thinking, she turned and fled.

Tink was sitting in the shade of a wild rosebush, deep in thought. She didn't notice Vidia, a fast-flying-talent fairy, flying overhead. Suddenly, Vidia landed right in front of Tink.

"Tinker Bell, darling," Vidia greeted her.

"Hello, Vidia," Tink replied. Of all the fairies in the kingdom, Vidia was the one Tink liked the least. Vidia was pretty, with her long dark hair, arched eyebrows, and pouting lips. But she was selfish and mean-spirited, and at the moment she was smiling in a way Tink didn't like at all.

"I'm so *sorry* to hear about your trouble, Tink darling," Vidia said.

"It's nothing," Tink said. "I was just flustered. I'll go back to the kitchen and fix the teakettle now."

"Oh, don't worry about that. Angus was in the tearoom," Vidia said. Angus was a pots-and-pans sparrow man. "He got the teakettle to shut up. No, Tink, what I meant was, I'm sorry to hear about your *talent*."

Tink blinked. "What do you mean?"

"Oh, don't you know?" Vidia asked. "Everyone's talking about it. The rumour flying around the kingdom, Tink dear, is that you've lost your talent."

"What?" Tink leaped to her feet.

"Oh, it's such a *shame*, dearest," Vidia went on, shaking her head. "You were always such a good little tinker."

"I haven't lost my talent," Tink growled. Her cheeks were burning. Her hands were balled into fists.

"If you say so. But, sweetheart, you have to admit, your work hasn't exactly been... *inspired* lately. Why, even I could fix pots and pans better than that," Vidia said with a little laugh. "But I wouldn't worry too much. I'm sure they won't make you leave the fairy kingdom *forever*, even if your talent has dried up for good."

Tink looked at her coldly. *I wish* you *would leave forever*, she thought. But she wasn't going to give Vidia the satisfaction of seeing that she was mad. Instead, she said, "I'm sure that would never happen, Vidia."

"Yes." Vidia gave Tink a pitying smile. "But no one really knows, do they? After all, no fairy has ever lost her talent before. But I guess we'll soon find out. You see, dear heart, I've come with a message. The queen would like to see you."

Tink's stomach did a little flip. The queen?

"She's in the gazebo," Vidia told her. "I'll let you fly there on your own. I expect you'll want to collect your thoughts. Goodbye, Tink." With a last sugary smile, Vidia flew away.

Tink's heart raced. What could this mean? Was it really possible that she could be banished from the kingdom for losing her talent?

But I haven't lost my talent! Tink thought indignantly. *I've just lost my hammer.*

With that thought in mind, Tink took a deep breath, lifted her chin, and flew off to meet the queen.

6

As she made her way to the gazebo, Tink passed a group of harvest-talent fairies filling wheelbarrows with sunflower seeds to take to the kitchen. They laughed and chatted as they worked, but as soon as they saw Tink, they all stopped talking. Silently, they watched her go by. Tink could have sworn she heard one of them whisper the word "talent."

So it's true, Tink thought. *Everyone is saying I've lost my talent.*

Tink scowled as she flew past another group of fairies who silently gawked at her. She had always hated gossip, and now she hated it even more.

The queen's gazebo sat high on a rock overlooking the fairy kingdom. Tink landed lightly on a bed of soft moss outside the entrance. All around her she heard the jingle of seashell wind chimes, which hung around the gazebo.

Inside, the gazebo was drenched in purple from the sunlight filtering through the violet petals that made up the roof. Soft, fresh fir needles carpeted the floor and gave off a piney scent.

Queen Ree stood at one of the open windows. She was looking out at the glittering blue water of the Mermaid Lagoon, which lay in the distance beyond the fairy kingdom. When she heard Tink, she turned.

"Tinker Bell, come in," said the queen.

Tink stepped inside. She waited.

"Tink, how are you feeling?" Queen Ree asked.

"I'm fine," Tink replied.

"Are you sleeping well?" asked the queen.

"Well enough," Tink told her. *Except for last night,* she added to herself. But she didn't feel the need to tell this to the queen.

"No cough? Your glow hasn't changed colour?" asked the queen.

"No," Tink replied. Suddenly, she realised that the queen was checking her for signs of fairy distemper. It was a rare illness, but very contagious. If Tink had it, she would have to be separated from the group to keep from making the whole fairy kingdom sick. "No, I'm fine," Tink repeated to reassure her. "I feel very well. Really."

When the queen heard this, she

seemed to relax. It was just the slightest change in her posture, but Tink noticed, and she, too, breathed a sigh of relief. Queen Ree would not banish her, Tink realised. The queen would never make such a hasty or unfair decision. It had been mean and spiteful of Vidia to say such a thing.

"Tink, you know there are rumours…" Queen Ree hesitated. She was reluctant to repeat them.

"They say I've lost my talent," Tink said quickly so that the queen wouldn't have to. "It's nasty gossip – and untrue. It's just that – " Tink stopped. She tugged at her fringe.

She was afraid that if she told Queen Ree about her missing hammer, the queen would think she was irresponsible.

Queen Ree waited for Tink to go on. When she didn't, the queen walked closer to her and looked into her blue eyes. "Tink," she said, "is there anything you want to tell me?"

She asked so gently that Tink felt the urge to plop down on the soft fir needles and tell her everything – about the pebble hammer and the carpenter's hammer and even about Peter Pan. But Tink had never told another fairy about Peter, and she was afraid to now.

Besides, Tink told herself, *the queen has more important things to worry about than a missing hammer.*

Tink shook her head. "No," she said. "I'm sorry my pots and pans haven't been very good lately. I'll try to do better."

Queen Ree looked carefully at her. She

knew something was wrong, but she didn't know what. She only knew that Tink didn't want to tell her. "Very well," she said. As Tink turned to leave, she added, "Be good to yourself, Tink."

Outside, Tink felt better. The meeting with the queen had been nothing to worry about at all. Maybe things weren't as bad as they seemed. *All I have to do now is find a new hammer, and everything will be back to normal,* Tink thought with a burst of confidence.

"Tink!" someone called.

She looked down and saw Rani and Prilla standing knee-deep in a puddle. Tink flew down and landed at the edge.

"What are you doing?" she asked, eyeing the fairies' wet clothes and hair. She was used to seeing Rani in the water. But Prilla wasn't a water fairy.

"Rani's showing me how she makes fountains in the water," Prilla explained. "I want to learn. I thought it might be fun to try in Clumsy children's lemonade." Prilla's talent was travelling over to the mainland in the blink of an eye and visiting the children there. She was the only fairy in all of Never Land who had this talent, and it was an important one. She helped keep up children's belief in fairies, which in turn saved the fairies' lives.

Tink looked at the drenched hem of Prilla's long dress and shivered. She didn't like to get wet – it always made her feel cold. She was surprised that Prilla could stand to be in the water for so long.

"I've been trying all afternoon, but this is all I can do," Prilla told her. She took a pinch of fairy dust and sprinkled it onto the water. Then she stared hard at the spot where the dust had landed and concentrated with all her might. After a moment, a few small bubbles rose to the surface and popped.

"Like a tadpole burping," Prilla said with a sigh. "Now watch Rani."

Rani sprinkled a pinch of fairy dust on the water, then stared at the spot where it had landed. Instantly, a twelve-inch fountain of water shot up from the puddle.

Tink and Prilla clapped their hands and cheered. "If I could make just a teeny little fountain, I'd be happy," Prilla confessed to Tink. Tink nodded, though she didn't really understand. She'd never wanted to make a water fountain.

Just then, Tink heard a snuffling sound. She turned and saw that Rani was crying.

"I'm so sorry, Tink," Rani said. She pulled a damp leafkerchief from one of her many pockets and blew her nose into it. As a water fairy, Rani cried a lot and was always prepared. "About your talent, I mean."

Tink's smile faded. She tugged at her fringe. "There's nothing to be sorry about. There's nothing wrong with my talent," she said irritably.

"Don't worry, Tink," Prilla said. "I know how you feel. When I thought I didn't have a talent, it was awful." Prilla hadn't known what her talent was when she first arrived in Never Land. She'd had to figure it out on her own. "Maybe you just need to try lots of things," she advised Tink, "and then it will come to you."

"I already have a talent, Prilla," Tink

said carefully.

"But maybe you need another talent, like a backup when the one you have isn't working," Prilla went on. "You could learn to make fountains with me. Rani will teach you, too, won't you, Rani?"

Rani sniffled helplessly. Tink tugged her fringe so hard that a few blonde hairs came out in her fingers. What Prilla was suggesting sounded crazy to Tink. She had never wanted to do anything but fix pots and pans.

"Anyway, Tink," said Prilla, "I wouldn't worry too much about what everyone is saying about – "

"Dinner?" Rani cut Prilla off.

Prilla looked at her. "No, I meant – "

"Yes, about dinner," Rani interrupted again, more firmly. She had dried her eyes and now she was looking hard at Prilla.

Rani could see that the topic of talents was upsetting Tink, and she wanted Prilla to be quiet. "It's time, isn't it?"

"Yes," said Tink. But she wasn't looking at Rani and Prilla. Her mind seemed to be somewhere else altogether.

Rani put her fingers to her mouth and whistled. They heard the sound of wings beating overhead. A moment later, Brother Dove landed on the ground next to Rani. He would take her to the tearoom.

But before Rani had even climbed onto his back, Tink took off in the direction of the Home Tree without another word. Rani and Prilla had no choice but to follow.

7

WHEN THEY REACHED the tearoom, Tink said goodbye to Rani and Prilla. Rani was going to sit with the other water-talent fairies, and Prilla was joining her. Since Prilla didn't have her own talent group, she was an honorary member of many different talents, and she sat at a different table every night. Tonight she would sit with the water-talent fairies and practice making fountains in her soup.

Tink made her way over to a table under a large chandelier where the pots-and-pans fairies sat together for their meals. As she took her seat, the other fairies at the table barely looked up.

"It's a crack in the bottom, I'll bet," a fairy named Zuzu was saying. "I mended a pewter bowl once that had had boiling water poured in it when it was cold. A crack had formed right down the centre." Her eyes glazed over happily as she recalled fixing the bowl.

"But don't you think it could be something around the drain, since the water leaked out so quickly?" asked Angus, the sparrow man who had fixed the whistling teakettle in the kitchen earlier that day.

A serving-talent fairy with a large soup tureen walked over to the table and began to ladle chestnut dumpling soup into the fairies' bowls. Tink noticed with pride that the ladle was one she had once repaired.

She leaned forward. "What's everyone talking about?" she asked the rest of the table.

The other fairies turned, as if noticing for the first time that Tink was sitting there.

"About Queen Ree's bathtub," Zuzu explained. "She's asked us to come fix it tomorrow. We're trying to guess what's wrong with it."

"Oh, yes!" said Tink. "I've been thinking about that, too. It might be a pinprick hole. Those are the sneakiest sorts of leaks – the water just sort of drizzles out one drop at a time." Tink laughed.

But no one joined her. She looked around the table. The other fairies were staring at her, or looking awkwardly down at their soup bowls. Suddenly, Tink realised that the queen had said nothing to her about the bathtub that afternoon in the gazebo.

"Tink," another fairy named Copper said gently, "we've all agreed that Angus and Zuzu should be the ones to repair the tub, since they are the most talented pots-and-pans fairies... lately, that is."

"Oh!" said Tink. "Of course." She swallowed hard. She felt as if a whole chestnut dumpling were stuck in her throat.

Now all the pots-and-pans fairies were looking at Tink with a mixture of love and concern. And, Tink was sad to see, pity.

I could just tell everyone that I lost my hammer, Tink thought. *But if they asked about the spare…*

Tink couldn't finish the thought. For a long, long time, Tink had neglected her pots and pans to spend all her time with Peter Pan. It was something she thought the other pots-and-pans fairies would never understand.

At last the fairies changed the topic and began to talk about the leaky pots and broken teakettles they'd fixed that day. As they chattered and laughed, Tink silently ate her soup.

Nearby, a cheer went up from the water fairies' table. Tink looked over and saw that Prilla had succeeded in making a tiny fountain in her soup.

Prilla has two talents now, Tink thought glumly. *And I haven't even got one.*

As soon as she was done with her soup, Tink put down her spoon and slipped away from the table. The other pots-and-pans fairies were so busy talking, they didn't notice her leaving.

Outside, Tink returned to the topmost branches of the Home Tree, where she'd sat the night before. She didn't want to go back to her workshop – there were pots and pans still waiting to be fixed. She didn't want to go to her room, either. It seemed too lonely there. At least here she had the stars to keep her company.

"Maybe it's true that I've lost my talent," Tink said to the stars. "If I don't have a hammer, then I can't fix things. And if I can't fix things, it's just like having no talent at all."

The stars only twinkled in reply.

From where she was sitting, Tink could see the hawthorn tree where Mother Dove lived. Between its branches, she could make out the faint shape of Mother Dove's nest. Mother Dove was the only creature in the fairy kingdom who knew all about Tink and Peter Pan. Once, after the hurricane that broke Mother Dove's wings and nearly destroyed Never Land, Tink had sat on the beach with Mother Dove and told her tales of her adventures with Peter. She had also told Mother Dove about the Wendy, and how when she came to Never Land, Peter forgot all about Tink.

What a comfort it would be to go to Mother Dove. She would know what to do.

But something held Tink back. She remembered Mother Dove's words to her on her very first day in Never Land: *You're Tinker Bell, sound and fine as a bell. Shiny and jaunty as a new pot. Brave enough for anything, the most courageous fairy to come in a long year.* Tink had felt so proud that day.

But Tink didn't feel very brave right now, certainly not brave enough to go to Peter's and get her spare hammer. He was only a boy, but still she couldn't find the courage.

Tink couldn't bear the idea that Mother Dove would think she wasn't brave or sound or fine. It would be worse than losing her talent.

"Tink," said a voice.

Tink turned. Terence was standing behind her on the branch. She'd been so wrapped up in her thoughts, she hadn't even heard him fly up.

"I haven't fixed the ladle yet," Tink told him miserably.

"I didn't come because of the ladle," Terence replied. "I saw you leave the tearoom."

When Tink didn't explain, Terence sat down next to her on the branch. "Tink, are you all right? Everyone is saying that... " He paused. Like Queen Ree, Terence couldn't bring himself to repeat the gossip. It seemed too unkind.

"That I've lost my talent," Tink finished for him. She sighed. "Maybe they're right, Terence. I can't seem to fix anything. Everything I touch comes out worse than when I started."

Terence was startled. One thing he had always admired about Tink was her fierceness: her fierce dark eyebrows, her fierce determination, even the fierce happiness of her dimpled smile. He had never seen her look as defeated as she did now.

"I don't believe that," he told her. "You're the best pots-and-pans fairy in the kingdom. Talent doesn't just go away like that."

Tink said nothing. But she felt grateful to him for not believing the rumours. For still believing in her.

"Tink," Terence asked gently, "what's really going on?"

Tink hesitated. "I lost my hammer," she blurted at last.

As soon as the words left her lips, Tink felt relieved. It was as if she'd let out a huge breath that she'd been holding in.

"Is that all it is?" Terence said. He almost laughed. It seemed like such a small thing. "But you could borrow a hammer," he suggested.

Tink told Terence about the hammer she'd made from a pebble and the one she'd borrowed from the carpenter fairy. "Neither of them works," she explained. "I need a tinker's hammer."

"Maybe there's a spare – " Terence began.

"I *have* a spare," Tink wailed. She'd already been over this so many times in her own mind. "But it's... I... I left it at Peter Pan's hideout."

"He won't give it back?" asked Terence.

Tink shook her head. "I haven't asked." She looked away.

Terence didn't know much about Peter Pan, only that Tink had been friends with him and then – suddenly – she wasn't. But he saw that Tink was upset and ashamed, and he didn't ask her anything more. Again, Tink felt a surge of gratitude toward him.

They sat silently for a moment, looking up at the stars.

"I could go with you," Terence said at last. "To Peter Pan's, I mean."

Tink's mind raced. Perhaps if someone

else came along, it wouldn't be so hard to see Peter...

"You would do that?" she asked.

"Tink," said Terence, "I'm your friend. You don't even need to ask."

He gave Tink a sparkling smile. This time, Tink saw it and she smiled back.

8

Early the next morning, before most of the fairy kingdom was awake, Tink rapped at the door of Terence's room. She wanted to leave for Peter's hideout before she lost her nerve altogether.

Terence threw open the door after the first knock. He grinned at Tink. "Ready to go get your talent back, Tinker Bell?"

Tink smiled. She was glad Terence was going with her, and not just because it would be easier with someone else along.

They left Pixie Hollow just as the sun's rays shone over Torth Mountain. They flew over the banana farms, where the Tiffens were already out working in the fields. In the distance, they could hear the laughter of the mermaids in the lagoon.

"See that peak?" Tink told Terence. She pointed out a chair-shaped spot at the top of a hill. "That's called the Throne. When the Lost Boys have their skirmishes, the winner is named king of the hill. Of course, if Peter is there, he always wins. The Lost Boys wouldn't dare to beat him, even if they could," Tink explained.

"And that stream," she went on, pointing to a silver ribbon of water winding through the forest below, "leads to an underground cavern that's filled with gold and silver. Captain Hook and his men have hidden away a whole pirate ship's worth of treasure there."

Tink remembered how she had found the cavern. She had been racing along the stream in a little birchbark canoe Peter had made for her. Peter had been running along the bank. When the stream suddenly dove underground, Tink had plunged right along with it. Peter had been so thrilled with her discovery that Tink hadn't even minded the soaking she got when the canoe splashed down in the cavern.

"You must know Never Land better than any fairy in the kingdom," Terence said admiringly.

Tink looked at the island below her and felt a little twinge of pride. What Terence said was true. With Peter, Tink had explored nearly every inch of Never Land. Every rock, meadow, and hill reminded her of some adventure.

Of course, they also reminded her of Peter.

Tink felt a flutter of nervousness. How would it be to see him? What if the

Wendy was there, or Peter had found someone else to play with? What if he ignored her again?

Tink fell silent. Terence, sensing that something bothered her, said nothing more for the rest of their trip.

When Tink reached the densest, darkest part of the forest, she began to glide down in a spiral. Terence followed her.

They plunged through a canopy of fig trees and landed on a white-speckled mushroom. The mushroom was nearly as wide as a Clumsy's dinner plate. Terence was surprised to feel that it was quite warm.

"It's Peter's hideout," Tink explained. "They use a mushroom cap to disguise the chimney to fool Captain Hook."

After they'd rested for a moment, Tink sprang from the mushroom and flew up to a hollow in the trunk of a nearby jackfruit tree. She was about to dive inside when Terence grabbed her wrist.

"What about owls?" he said worriedly. If there was an owl living in the hollow, it might eat them.

Tink laughed. "Anything that lived here would be terrorised by the Lost Boys. This is the entrance to the hideout!"

Peeking inside, Terence saw the entire tree was hollow, right to its roots. He followed Tink as she flew down the trunk. They came out in an underground room.

Terence looked around. The floor and walls were made of packed earth. Tree roots hung down from the ceiling, and from these, string hammocks dangled limply. Here and there on the ground lay slingshots, socks, and dirty coconut-shell bowls. The remains of a fire smoldered in a corner. The whole place had the dry, puppyish smell of little boys.

But there were no little boys in sight. The hideout was empty.

He's not home, Tink thought. She felt both disappointed and relieved.

Just then, they heard whistling coming from somewhere near the back of the den.

Tink and Terence flew toward the sound. Their glows made two bright spots of light in the dim room.

At the back of the hideout, they spied a nook that was tucked out of sight from the rest of the room. The whistling was coming from there.

When they rounded the corner, Terence saw a freckled boy with a mop of red hair sitting on a stool formed by a thick, twisted root. In one hand he held a jackknife, and he whistled as he worked it over a piece of wood. A fishing pole leaned against the wall behind him. Looking more closely, Terence saw that the boy was carving a fishing hook big enough to catch a whale.

Tink saw her old friend, Peter Pan.

Taking a deep breath, Tink said, "Hello, Peter."

But Peter didn't seem to hear her. He continued to whistle and chip at the wood.

Tink flew a little bit closer. "Peter!" she exclaimed.

Peter kept on whistling and whittling.

Was he deaf? Or could he be angry with her? Tink wondered with a sudden shock. The thought had never occurred to her. She hovered, unsure what to do.

Then Terence took her hand. They

flew up to Peter until they were just a few inches from his face. "Peter!" they both cried.

Peter lifted his head. When he saw them, a bright smile lit his face.

Tink smiled, too.

"Hello! What's this?" Peter said. He looked back and forth between the fairies. "Two butterflies have come to visit me! Are you lost, butterflies?"

Tink's smile faded. She and Terence stared at Peter. *Butterflies?*

Tink thought, *Has he forgotten me already?*

Peter squinted at them and whistled low. "You're awful pretty. I just love butterflies," he said. "You'd make a fine addition to my collection. Let's see now, where are my pins?"

He began to search his pockets. As he did, small items fell onto the ground beneath his seat: a parrot's feather, a snail shell, a bit of string.

"Here it is!" he cried. He held up a straight pin with a coloured bulb on the end. It was big enough to skewer a butterfly – or a fairy – right through the middle.

"Now hold still," Peter said. Gripping the pin in one hand, he reached up to grab Tink and Terence with the other.

"Fly!" Terence screamed to Tink.

Just before Peter's stubby fingers closed around them, the fairies turned and fled toward the exit.

BUT AS THEY reached the roots of the jackfruit tree, they heard a whoop of laughter behind them.

Tink stopped and glanced back over her shoulder. Peter was clutching his stomach and shaking with laughter.

"Oh, Tink!" he gasped. "You should have seen the looks on your faces. Butterflies! Oh, I am funny. Oh, oh." He bent over as another round of laughter seized him.

Terence, who had been just ahead of Tink, also stopped and turned. Frowning, he came to hover next to her. He had never met Peter Pan face to face before, and he was starting to think that he wasn't going to like him very much.

But Tink was smiling. It had only been a joke! Peter *did* remember her!

At last Peter stopped laughing. He bounded up to Tink and Terence, his eyes shining.

"Tink!" he cried. "It's awful great to see you. Where've you been hiding?"

"Hello, Peter," Tink replied. "Meet my friend Terence."

"A boy pixie! Fantastic!" Peter cried, turning to stare at Terence.

The grin on his face was so wide and enthusiastic that Terence's heart softened. The thing was, it was impossible not to like Peter Pan. He had the eagerness of a puppy, the cleverness of a fox, and the freedom of a lark – all rolled into one spry, redheaded boy.

"You'll never guess what I've got, Tink.

Come see!" He said it as if Tink had been away for a mere few hours and had now come back to play.

Peter led Tink and Terence over to a corner of the hideout and pulled a wooden cigar box out of a hole in the wall. The word "Tarantula" was burned onto the lid. It was the name of the cigars Captain Hook liked to smoke. Peter had found the empty box on the beach, where Hook had thrown it away.

"I keep my most important things in my treasure chest," Peter explained to Terence, gesturing to the box. "The Lost Boys know better than to go poking around in here."

"Where are the Lost Boys?" Tink asked.

Peter thought for a moment. "They

must still be hiding," he replied finally. "We were playing hide-and-seek in the forest yesterday. But when it was my turn to look, I spotted a bobcat stalking a rabbit. Course, I wanted to see if he caught him, so I followed them. I guess I forgot to go back and look for the boys."

"Do you think they're lost?" Terence asked.

Peter grinned. "Course they're lost! They're the Lost Boys! I'll go find them later." He shrugged, then added, "Anyway, that bobcat never did catch the rabbit."

Peter lifted the lid of the cigar box. "Now . . ." Reaching inside, he took out a small object. He held it out toward Tink and Terence in the palm of his hand. It was yellowish white and shaped like a triangle, with razor-sharp edges that narrowed to a point.

Tink clasped her hands together. "Oh!" she gasped. "You got it!"

"What is it?" Terence asked.

"A shark's tooth," Peter replied, just a bit smugly. "Isn't it swell? I'm going to put it on a string and make a necklace."

"The first time I met Peter, he was trying to steal a shark's tooth," Tink explained to Terence.

"That's right!" exclaimed Peter. "I'd made a bet with the boys that I could steal a tooth from a live shark. I built a small raft out of birchwood and was paddling out to sea... "

From the way he began, Terence could tell that Peter had told this story many times before, and that he loved telling it.

"I had just paddled beyond the reef,"

Peter continued, "when I felt something bump the underside of my raft."

"The shark?" asked Terence.

Peter nodded. "He was looking for his lunch. But he didn't know that I was looking for him, too!"

"How did you plan to get his tooth?" Terence asked.

"I meant to stun him with my oar, then steal the tooth while he was out cold," said Peter. "But he was bigger than I'd thought, and before I knew it, he'd bitten my little raft right in half! I was sinking fast, and it looked like the end for me, when suddenly I heard a jingling sound over my head. I looked up and there was Tinker Bell. She yelled down at me . . ."

"'Fly, silly boy!'" Tink and Peter cried together. They laughed, remembering.

"But I didn't know how to fly," Peter told Terence. "So Tink taught me how, right then and there. She sprinkled some fairy dust on me, and before I knew it, I'd zipped up into the air, out of the shark's reach. Boy, was he mad!"

"So, you went back and got the shark tooth this time?" Tink asked Peter, pointing to the tooth in his hand.

Peter shrugged. "Naw. A mermaid gave this to me. But now I'm going to go out and get the whole shark!" He pointed to the fishing pole and the wooden hook he'd been carving.

Tink and Peter both burst out laughing.

Terence smiled, watching them. He felt glad that Tink looked so happy. But it also made him sad. What if she decided to stay here in the forest with Peter?

Tink *was* happy. She had discovered that it wasn't so hard to see Peter, after all! She'd only needed a friend to help her find that out. She saw Terence's smile, and she smiled back at him.

Just then, Tink caught sight of something in the cigar box. Her eyes widened. "My hammer!" she exclaimed.

"I saved it for you, Tink," Peter said proudly. "I knew you'd be back for it."

Tink reached into the box and picked up the hammer. It fit perfectly in her hand. She tapped it lightly into the palm of her other hand, then closed her eyes and sighed. She felt as if she'd come home after a long, long trip.

Then, to Terence's joy and relief, Tink turned to Peter and said, "It's been so good to see you, Peter. But we have to go back to the fairy kingdom now."

Peter looked at her in surprise. "What? Now? But what about hide-and-seek?"

Tink shook her head. She was glad to realize that she didn't want to stay, not for hide-and-seek or anything else. She wanted to get back to Pixie Hollow, back to her pots and pans. That was where she belonged.

Tink flew so close to Peter's face that he had to cross his eyes to see her. She kissed the bridge of his freckled nose. "I'll come back soon to visit," she promised. And she meant it.

Then, taking Terence's hand, she flew back out of the jackfruit tree and into the forest.

As Tink headed back to the fairy kingdom with Terence, one last thing was bothering her.

She didn't want all of Pixie Hollow to know about the hammer and her trip to see Peter. Enough hurtful gossip had already spread through the kingdom. Tink didn't want any more.

She wanted to ask Terence if he would keep their trip to Peter's a secret between them. But before she could, he turned to her. "I don't think anyone else needs to know about this trip, do you?" he asked. "You've got your hammer back, and that's what matters."

Tink grinned and nodded. What a good friend Terence was.

"The only thing is," Terence said, "how will we convince everyone that you have your talent back?"

Tink thought for a moment. "I have an idea," she said.

Putting on a burst of speed, Tink raced Terence all the way back to Pixie Hollow.

When they got to the Home Tree, Tink went straight to Queen Ree's quarters.

One of the queen's attendants opened the door. "Tink, welcome," the attendant said when she saw her.

"I've come to fix the queen's bathtub," Tink told her.

Terence, who was standing behind Tink, grinned. Tink was clever. This was the perfect way to prove that her talent was back. Terence didn't doubt that Tink could fix the tub. She was the best pots-and-pans fairy in the kingdom.

But the attendant hesitated. Everyone had heard about Tink and her talent. She wanted to refuse to let Tink fix it.

Just then, Ree stepped forward. She had heard Tink's request. "Come in, Tink," she said.

"I've come to fix your bathtub," Tink repeated to the queen.

Ree looked at Tink. In Tink's blue eyes, she saw a fierce certainty that hadn't been there the day before, when they'd talked in the gazebo.

Ree nodded. "Take Tink to the bathtub," she told her attendant.

The attendant looked startled, but she turned and began to lead Tink away.

Just before Tink left, Terence grabbed her hand. "Good luck," he said.

Tink held up her hammer and gave his hand a squeeze. "I don't need it!" she said.

Join Tinker Bell, Prilla and all
the other Never Fairies in
the next Disney Fairies book...

Lily's Pesky Plant

Here is a fairy-sized preview
of the first chapter!

Lily's Pesky Plant

1

EARLY ONE MORNING, Lily woke to the sound of birds chirping in the topmost branches of the Home Tree, the ancient maple where Never Land's fairies live. Opening her eyes, she saw the walls of her room stretch ever so slightly as the great tree reached its branches toward the early morning sun. Lily pushed back her fern frond quilt and yawned, stretching her arms up into the air.

Lily climbed out of bed and opened the doors of her wardrobe, which was made from a dried gourd. She chose a thistledown shirt and knickers woven from dandelion fluff. Unlike some fairies, Lily didn't like spider-silk gowns and shoes with heels as thin as pine needles. She liked simple, sturdy clothes.

In the tearoom, Lily had her usual breakfast, a cup of lemongrass tea and a slice of poppy seed cake. Some of the other garden-talent fairies at Lily's table sat for a while at breakfast. They refilled their pots of tea and spread heaps of black cherry jam on their bread. But not Lily. The moment her plate and cup were empty, she pushed them aside and flew off to her garden.

Lily's garden was just two frog's leaps beyond the Home Tree, right in the heart of Pixie Hollow. All the fairies agreed that it was one of the nicest places in the entire fairy kingdom. On one side of her garden was a hedge of raspberry bushes. On the other side, a wild rosebush sweetly scented the air. Everywhere bright red and orange poppies sprang from the ground. Clusters of Queen Anne's lace and lilac made pleasant groves where a fairy could sit and think. And throughout the garden, sweet clover sprouted in fairy-sized beds. They were perfect for taking naps in.

The garden was a favourite spot of many fairies, who were always dropping by. Harvest-talent fairies picked raspberries from the bushes. Healing-talent fairies collected herbs for their potions. Other fairies simply liked to walk among the beautiful flowers.

Lily welcomed them all. Next to working in her garden, Lily's favourite thing was watching fairies enjoy the beautiful plants she grew. The fairies also enjoyed Lily's company. With her friendly, direct smile and her sparkling dark eyes, she was as fresh and lovely as the flowers she grew.

As soon as Lily got to her garden, she called out, "Bumble!" At once, a large bee zipped out of the flowers and flew up to her. Bumble was yellow, round, and fuzzy all over. He wasn't Lily's pet, exactly. He had just showed up one day and never left. The two had become good friends.

Bumble always followed Lily as she took care of her plants. She watered them. She checked their leaves for spots. That morning Lily saw that some of the daffodils had been toppled by a breeze. She tied the stems to stakes to help them stand sturdy and strong again.

When she was done making the rounds in her garden, Lily lay down on a patch of soft moss to watch the grass grow. To you this might sound boring, but for her it was every bit as exciting as watching butterfly races (a favourite fairy pastime). Lily was certain that the blades of grass grew faster when they knew she was watching.

Unluckily for Lily, she was the only fairy in all of Pixie Hollow to have this hobby. When others saw her lying in the grass, they usually thought she was doing nothing at all. Often, they would start talking to her. This frustrated Lily, for it broke her concentration.

And that was exactly what happened that morning. Bumble was buzzing around the buttercups in the corner of her garden, and Lily was lying nearby, watching a (very slow) race between two blades of grass. One blade was winning, and Lily was urging the other one to catch up, when a voice broke through her thoughts.

"I say, what a funny thing!" The voice

was loud and a bit shrill.

Lily didn't move, except to lower her eyelids. She hoped whoever it was would think she was sleeping and go away.

"I said, what a funny thing!" the voice cried, even more shrilly.

Lily sighed and opened her eyes. A tall fairy was standing over her. She had curly hair the colour of a wax bean and a long, narrow nose that was red at the tip.

"Hello, Iris," said Lily, sitting up. "What's so funny?"

"Why, just look at your buttercups."

Lily looked. She didn't see anything funny about them.

"They're the biggest I've ever seen!" Iris exclaimed. "You ought to call them butter-*bowls* instead." She chuckled at her own joke.

Lily smiled politely. "They do seem

happy," she replied. Lily didn't care how big or small a plant was, as long as it was happy. That was the reason the plants in her garden grew so well – she made sure they were all content.

"Of course, they're nothing like the buttercups I used to grow," Iris went on. "They were as big as soup pots and yellow as the sun. I'll tell you a secret I learned from a Tiffen: you have to give them *real butter*."

Lily raised her eyebrows in surprise. The Tiffens were big-eared creatures who grew bananas. Their farms weren't far from Pixie Hollow. Lily had never heard of a Tiffen who grew buttercups.

Then again, she thought, *what do I know about Tiffens?* Lily didn't spend very much time outside her garden.

Iris gave her a smug little nod. Like

Lily, Iris was a garden-talent fairy. She had once had her own garden, but it was so long ago no one could remember what it had been like.

Then Iris had begun writing her plant book. Now, she claimed, she was much too busy to do any real gardening. Instead, she went around poking her nose into other fairies' gardens. She said she was collecting information for her book. But she usually did more talking than listening.

Lily couldn't imagine what it would be like to be a garden fairy without a garden. She thought it must be awful.

Iris plopped down on a spotted red toadstool and flipped open the birch bark cover of her book. She turned its pages, which were made from leaves. Iris carried the book with her everywhere she went.

"Anyway, Lily," Iris said, "I've come because I'm worried about your snapdragons. Now, don't get me wrong. They seem perfectly healthy and strong. But when I went to take a peek at their petals the other day, one snapped at me!"

"They're *snap*dragons, Iris," Lily pointed out patiently. "It's their nature to be cranky."

"Well, I *know* a thing or two about snapdragons, Lily," Iris said. "And you can't just let them act wild. You've got to *train* them." Iris continued to flip through the pages of her book. "I found a perfectly brilliant way to keep them from snapping." She tapped the page she'd opened to. "Here, I'll read it to you. 'A Cure for Snappish Snapdragons, by Iris. If your snapdragons have bad manners, you must pinch their leaves whenever they snap at you... '"

As Iris read on, Lily's toes began to wiggle impatiently. Suddenly, she blurted out, "Actually, Iris, I was just about to leave."

It wasn't true, and Lily wasn't quite sure why she'd said it. She knew Iris only meant to be helpful. But maybe she was annoyed with Iris for interrupting her peaceful morning. Or maybe it was just that Lily *liked* her snapdragons to be snappish. Whatever the reason, on this particular day, Lily just didn't feel like listening to Iris.

"Where are you going? I could come with you and tell you more on the way," Iris offered.

"Oh, but... I'm going fern spotting. Possum ferns, that is," Lily said quickly. Any fairy knew it was impossible to look for possum ferns and talk at the same time. The ferns were shy and would wilt completely if they heard a noise.

"Oh. Okay, then. Another time." Iris blew her nose into a leafkerchief. She looked disappointed, and Lily felt a little pang. She wished she hadn't lied about going to the forest. But it was too late to take it back now.

"Yes, another time. See you, Iris," Lily said. She rose into the air and flew off into the forest.

When she was just out of sight from the garden, Lily landed near the roots of an old oak tree.

"I'll just go for a short walk," she told herself as she set out along a narrow path through the bushes. "Then I'll go back." She figured Iris would have moved to someone else's garden by then.

Most fairies never went to the forest alone because of snakes, owls, and hawks. And fairies almost never walked unless their wings were too wet to fly. But Lily was brave, and what was more, she liked walking. She felt closer to the plants when her feet were on the ground.

Lily walked along the forest floor. She kept an eye out for snakes. High above, the wind rustled the leaves of the trees. Lily took off her shoes. She liked the feeling of the damp soil between her toes.

Just then, she spotted something curled against the base of a rock. It was a silvery green plant with tightly coiled, velvety leaves. Lily smiled.

"A possum fern!" she whispered. She had spotted one after all! Holding her breath, Lily silently crept toward the rare plant to get a closer look.

Suddenly, something crashed through the leaves over her head. Lily gasped and flew for cover between the roots of a nearby tree. Had a hawk just swooped at her? Trembling, she peered out from behind the root and scanned the forest.

But there was no sign of a hawk. The forest was still and quiet. Lily looked over at the possum fern and saw that its leaves had uncoiled and turned brown. It had heard the noise and was playing dead.

Then Lily saw something that made her gasp again. In the spot where she had just been standing lay a strange seed.

Collect all the Disney Fairies books

Discover the story of the Never Fairies in Fairy Dust and the Quest for the Egg

Coming soon!